and the
Tunnel of Doom

Ailsa Wild

with illustrations by
BEN WOOD

raintree
a Capstone company — publishers for children

For Rainer, Nelleke and Anouk
who will read them together.
And for Emmaline, who
would have loved to.
– Ailsa

For Lauren, the **BEST** Taylor!
– Ben

Chapter One

"Messy, here boy!" I say. "Come *on*, Messy, this way."

I'm looking over my shoulder as I bolt away, slapping my leg and calling like crazy. Messy is running towards me, his tongue lolling, looking so happy. He's in **terrible danger**, and he has no idea. The only way I can keep him safe is if he obeys me *completely*.

"You can do it, Messy! Get out of there!"

He's super fast. Much faster than a kid. But he's easily distracted. He turns and sees who's following him. Then he heads straight towards the danger.

He collides with Vee's legs, and they both tumble on the grass. They roll over each other, a tangle of kid and puppy.

"OK, fine." I laugh and flop on the grass. "You tagged him, you win."

Vee is one of my bonus sisters. I call them that because they're the bonus I got when I moved in with my dad and their mum. My other bonus sister, Jessie, is lying in the shade by the climbing frame. She hates running. She's Vee's twin, but they're pretty much opposites.

Vee is giggling under a tangle of puppy. She pats him, and he squirms happily.

I scramble up. "My turn to be it!" I shout, running towards them.

Vee leaps to her feet and bolts away with Messy at her heels.

We're playing **Dog Tag**, which is a game I invented. The *it* person has to catch Messy, but they aren't allowed to call him *at all*. Everyone else is trying to get Messy away from the *it* person any way they can.

It's a weirdly hot afternoon. The hottest it's been in a long time. We're on the grass near our playground. Our park has a climbing frame part and a grass part. You're supposed to have dogs on their leads, so Messy's got a lead, but no one's holding onto it. It's trailing along the grass while Messy runs beside Vee.

I've almost caught up to them now. I can run faster than Vee, so as long as Messy stays with her, it'll be easy.

Then Jessie calls, "Messy!" from over at the bench.

Oh. Messy turns and bolts towards her.

We let Jessie do this because it makes the game more fun. She always chooses the right moment.

"Good *boy*, Messy!" she says, reaching into her pocket. She's more organized than us, so she always has doggy treats. Messy loves her.

Messy isn't our dog – we look after him for someone else. Her name is Carmeline Clancy, and she's a **film-star rock-climber** we made friends with. She lives in a no-pets hotel, and sometimes she's too busy filming to play with Messy. So we pick him up from his puppy boarding kennel and take him to the park after school some days.

Playing with Messy is the best. I chase after him, watching his tail wag in the air. But before I get there, Vee calls from another corner of the playground. Messy bolts towards her. Annoying! I'm so hot and out of breath. Also I want to win.

There's a stick on the ground just below me. Like a ninja, I pick it up while I'm still running. I don't even slow down. Then I wave it invitingly over my head. Will Messy see? He does. He gives a big doggy grin and starts puppy-dancing towards me.

"Squishy, that's cheating!" Vee says, slowing down as she gets closer.

Squishy – that's me. My real name is Sita, after my gran, but everyone calls me Squishy.

"There's no rule about sticks," I say as Messy tumbles into me.

It's true, we never *said* there was a rule about sticks. But we probably should have. I feel a **tiny twinge** of guilt, but mostly I just see the sweet, jumpy puppy around my knees and have the good feeling of winning.

"That win doesn't count," Vee says in her whiny voice.

"Cheating makes it less fun for everybody," says Jessie. As if she's ever played a game in her life. She's only older than Vee by forty-seven minutes, but sometimes she acts like she's our mum.

"OK, whatever," I say. "I'll still be it."

I lift the stick high over my head and throw it as far as I can. It circles in the blue sky, and Messy bolts. His legs are so fast, they're like a **cartoon** blur.

There's a little patch of taller grass near the corner. Past that, there's a little more mown grass and then the fence. The stick lands on the other side of the tall grass. Messy's bolting towards the stick, and I'm pounding behind him. He runs straight for the tall grass, pushing through it like it's not even there. But he doesn't come out the other side.

He should only have been in that grass for a second. **Where is he?**

I sprint towards the long grass and then stumble to a halt. The long grass is in a circle around a hole. A really deep hole – so dark that I can't see the bottom.

And Messy has fallen in.

Chapter Two

"**Messy!**" I shout, half-crying, half-calling him.

"Stop cheating, Squishy! You're not allowed to call him!" Vee shouts, running up behind me. Then, "Oh," as she sees what I'm seeing.

The metal cover that's supposed to be over the hole is pushed to the side. It's still half-over, enough to stop a person falling in. But not a puppy.

I kneel on the edge and lean my head in. "Messy?" I call. My voice sounds hollow, echoing back up at me. I listen. But there's nothing.

My heart drops into my shoes.

A whimpering little howl drifts up out of the darkness.

"Oh, Messy, you're alive!"

But he sounds like he's hurt. Messy isn't even our dog. What will Carmeline Clancy think if we let him get hurt?

There's a metal ladder going down into the dark.

"We have to get to him," I say, trying to push the cover aside. It's heavy. Vee kneels beside me, her face all red from running. We both try to push, but it doesn't budge. It's much too heavy.

I can hear Jessie walking towards us. "Squishy, what happened? Where's Messy?" Her feet stop by my knee. "**Oh no**."

Messy whimpers again, calling for me to help.

"Come on," I say. "Together."

Vee pushes. I push. Jessie stands, frozen, watching us. The cover doesn't move. Not even a fraction of a millimetre.

"Jessie?" I ask.

She blinks and then kneels beside us to push. The cover finally budges a tiny bit. We move it a centimetre at a time. I count, "Three, two, *one*," and we heave together, like **pirates** pulling ropes on a pirate ship. "Three, two, *one*." Breathe. "Three, two, *one*."

Finally there's enough room for me to squeeze in. I sit on the edge, find my footing on the ladder, and ease myself down.

"Squishy, what are you doing?" Jessie asks.

"I'm going to rescue him," I say.

Jessie's voice gets firmer. "But you can't go down there," she says.

Typical Jessie. Telling people what they can't do when it's a matter of life or death.

Messy's yodelling whimpers float up, sounding so sad it makes my heart hurt.

"Watch me," I say to Jessie, squeezing my hips down past the lid.

It's much cooler in the hole. Cold air flows over my legs in the darkness, while my face is still hot in the sun. The ladder is rusty and scratchy on my hands.

Once my shoulders are in, it's easy. I go faster but not too fast. I'm not totally reckless. I still have to feel for every foothold.

As I climb, I talk to Messy. "It's OK, I'm coming. You'll be all right."

He becomes more **frantic** as I get closer.

"Squishy, are you OK?" Vee calls, her voice sounding hollow and frightened.

"I'm almost there," I shout back up.

It's cold down here. Such a long way for a puppy to fall.

Finally, my foot finds solid ground instead of a ladder rung. I'm careful not to step on Messy.

"Hello, boy, here I am."

Why isn't Messy already leaping all over me? Is he hurt that badly? It's so dark that it's hard to see, but my eyes are slowly adjusting. Messy is just to one side of me, lying at a strange angle on the floor. I imagine all his legs being broken from the fall. What if he has to have casts on them for months? What will Carmeline Clancy say when I tell her?

"Are you at the bottom yet?" Jessie calls down.

"Yes, but something's wrong with Messy."

"I'm coming down," Vee says. I hear Jessie telling her not to, but she does anyway. It gets darker as her legs swing into the hole.

I crouch down next to Messy. He's scrabbling with his two front legs, which don't look very broken. But I can only really see half of him. There's something wrong with his back legs and tail. I squint and look closer. He's stuck under something.

There's a crack in the floor, and Messy's back legs are stuck in it. He must have been trying to scramble out and got himself caught. I tug him gently. He whimpers, but I give a little jiggle and his legs pull free.

"Is he OK?" Vee asks, landing with a loud thump on the ground beside me.

"I think he's fine." I stroke my hands down his back legs.

Messy wriggles and licks my face,

yapping happily. It makes me giggle. "He's fine," I say.

I put him on the ground to check if he can stand on his legs. And Messy **charges off** into the darkness, trailing his lead behind him.

Chapter Three

As soon as I see Messy's tail disappearing, I realize we're not just in a hole. We're in a tunnel.

"**Messy, wait!**" I shout.

"What's going on?" Jessie calls down.

I don't answer. I'm already following Messy. I can't actually run, because it's too dark to really see. But it's not pitch-black. There's a little bit of light ahead, as well as behind.

I hear Vee shouting up to Jessie. "We'll just be a minute, Jessie! Don't go anywhere." Then her footsteps trot behind me.

"Messy!" I call. "Here, boy. Come on, Messy!"

His claws skitter on the concrete ahead. We're on a narrow walkway with a wall on my right. On my left there's a river. Well, it's not really a river because there's not enough water for that. It's more like a stream. In the darkness it looks black and slimy.

"A whole tunnel, under the city!" Vee says.

The air smells like mud and moss. It's awesome.

Or it would be if we hadn't lost a puppy.

"Messy!" I call. *"Messy!"*

Up ahead there's a patch of light, maybe from another hole? Messy has paused there and is looking back at us, tongue lolling. I'm so relieved he hasn't totally disappeared.

"Messy!" I call and run up to him. But as soon as I'm close, he bolts away. He thinks we're playing tag again.

I stop. Chasing him isn't going to work. I wish we had Jessie's treats.

"That's the street," Vee says, standing in the light and looking up. There's a metal grate and busy feet crossing it. We're not under the playground any more.

"I wonder where this tunnel goes?" I think aloud.

It's heading downhill.

"Jessie will be worried," Vee says. But I can tell she wants to explore.

I say, "We can't leave Messy down here."

Vee nods seriously. Then we both grin and head into the darkness.

Messy stays ahead of us, but not too far ahead. The floor is a little slippery, and in some places it's really dark.

"This is actually the best," Vee says.

I agree. "You can totally imagine some kind of creepy, scaly monster living down here," I say.

Vee slows down. "Do you think there might be?"

Vee's funny like that. She's not scared of climbing high things or walking for miles in a dark tunnel. But as soon as you add creepy imaginings, she freaks out. She's scared of ghosts, even though they aren't real.

Soon the tunnel opens up into a cavern. There are more metal grates in the ceiling high above our heads, giving us a little bit of light.

"**Whoa!**" Vee says, and her voice booms strangely.

Our slimy little stream joins two others coming out of other tunnels. They all flow together down another tunnel. To our right there's a massive pile of something looming in the corner. I think it looks a bit like a curled-up monster, but I don't say that to Vee because I don't want her to freak out. Messy is sitting in the middle of the floor with his tail wagging like crazy.

This time I don't chase him. "Come on, boy," I say quietly and pat my knee. He looks. Then he stands up and trots towards me.

I pick Messy up and cuddle him. His fur tickles my cheek as I follow Vee out into the cavern.

"What's that pile?" I ask. As we get closer, I realize it's covered in some kind of orange plastic and tied down tight. Anyway, it's too dark to really see much.

"We should get back to Jessie," Vee says, sounding like she doesn't really want to.

I sort of want to explore more, but I know she's right. "Yeah, any minute now she'll probably freak out and run to get Dad and Alice," I say. Alice is my bonus sisters' mum, which makes her my bonus mum.

"She'd probably skip them and go straight to the police," Vee suggests.

I giggle. "Or the fire brigade, ambulance *and* emergency rescue people."

Vee cracks up. We're both laughing as we head back to our tunnel. Messy is wriggling in my arms trying to get free, so I find the end of his lead, wrap it tightly around my wrist, and put him down on the ground. He tries to go back towards the cavern, so I give his lead a little tug. He whines and comes with us.

"Actually Jessie's probably Googling all the different types of rescuers," Vee says. It makes us both laugh because

Jessie loves Google.

We walk and walk and walk. After a while, Vee says, "This is taking forever!"

As soon as she says it, I realize something I should have noticed when we left the cave.

"We're going downhill," I say. "The same direction as the stream!"

"But we were going downhill on the way in!" Vee says.

We stand and stare at each other in the dark. We must have taken the **wrong tunnel.**

Chapter Four

We have to turn around and go back. And when we get to the cavern, we have to work out which is the right tunnel to take us to the playground. By now Jessie is definitely freaking out. I wish we could tell her we're OK.

I squeeze Messy's lead tighter. He **dances** on the end of it. He knew we should have been going the other way – he tried to tell us.

"Isn't it lighter around the corner up there?" Vee says.

She's right. It *is* lighter ahead. A lot lighter. Messy starts tugging me towards the light, his happy tail wagging.

"It's probably another way out," says Vee.

When we turn the corner, there's daylight. Not shining down from a grate in the ceiling, but a whole round green circle of daylight. Green because it's surrounded by plants. Vee runs to the end, and I follow her, clutching Messy's lead. We stand at the edge of the tunnel. We're at the river.

Messy leaps around happily, barking as though we'd been underground for days instead of just a few minutes.

The city's river is wide and brown, flowing past us. Our slimy little stream is dribbling into it. We're standing on a weedy patch of grass. The tunnel comes out of a concrete wall behind us with a paved path running along the top of it. People are walking and cycling up there, and the city is just behind them.

"There's a *secret tunnel*, from *our* park to the *river*," I say, in a **mini-scream**.

We stop and look at each other. Vee's eyes are so bright and shining. "This is amazing, amazing, amazing!" she says. Her voice gets higher and higher with each "**amazing**", and Messy barks along with her. Then we are laughing and high-fiving, and Messy is jumping up, trying to catch our high fives.

Suddenly Vee stops. "We really have to go back."

It's hard to remember how worried Jessie will be, because *we* know we're OK.

I look up at the path, with the city behind it. "Which way do you think we should go?" I ask. "The streets or the tunnel?"

It's hard to decide.

"We-ell," Vee says. "Mum doesn't like it when we cross streets on our own."

I nod. We don't have to cross any streets to get from our apartment to the playground, which is why we're allowed to walk there alone.

"It's probably safer to go through the tunnel," I say seriously.

"Much safer," Vee agrees.

It's so good when the **safe choice** is also the **fun choice**. We head back into the darkness with Messy trotting in front.

When we get to the cavern, we pause.

"Which one?" Vee asks.

All the other tunnels are going uphill. It looks like they've joined here to go down to the river.

"Not that one," I say, pointing. "We would have had to cross the water to get out. I think we would have noticed that."

"And not that one," Vee says, "because the path's on the right of the stream."

She's right. There's only one choice. We start walking. But Messy doesn't move.

The fur around his shoulders is **spiky**, and he's starting to growl.

"What is it, boy?" I ask.

Then I hear footsteps. Loud, echoey, grown-up footsteps, coming down one of the other tunnels.

"**Hey!**" a man shouts. He sounds angry, and the footsteps get faster. I can see a light beam bouncing off the walls of the tunnel with the water crossing it.

"What are you kids *doing*?" He sounds so mean. It's like a monster's growl, and it booms through the tunnels.

"Run!" I shriek.

We race down our tunnel. Messy pulls me, running faster than both of us. Vee climbs the ladder first. I've never seen her climb so fast in my life.

When she's close to the top, she swings her legs up and reaches down for Messy. I climb a few steps one-handed, with Messy under my arm, then pass him up to her.

We scramble out into the sun. Messy jumps around happily, as though he's never seen daylight before. Jessie is nowhere to be seen.

"Quick, pretend we're in the middle of a game!" Vee says. Luckily there are about twenty kids in the playground now. We sit down opposite each other and start a clapping game. Hopefully the man won't even suspect us. We're suddenly clapping-game kids. Not exploring-secret-tunnels-under-the-city kids. Right?

The growly man climbs up out of the tunnel. He's wearing a neon orange top with a circle logo on his chest. He looks around the park suspiciously.

Eventually he shrugs and climbs back down into the hole. **Phew**.

Jessie and Dad come running into the park. She spots us first and bolts towards us. For someone who doesn't like sport, she can run pretty fast.

"You're OK! You're OK," Jessie says. "I thought something terrible had happened."

"We're fine," I say as we scramble to our feet.

Jessie whispers, "I didn't tell Tom about the tunnel, because I didn't want to scare him if you were OK."

"*Thank you.*" I'm so grateful I want to hug her.

Dad strides over. His mouth is in a firm line, and his eyes are **narrow— angry**. And he doesn't even know about the hole yet.

"What's going on?" he asks. "Where did you go?"

I glance at Vee. What should we tell him?

Chapter Five

"I promise we didn't cross over any streets," I say. I'm using my most sincere voice, because it's actually true. We didn't cross *over* any streets.

Dad has his stern voice on. "You scared Jessie so badly she came home," he says. "I don't care what you did or didn't do."

"But we–" I start.

"No buts, Sita," he says, holding up his hand. (Sita is my name for when I'm in

big trouble. And for the register at school.)
"I am seriously considering whether to let you come to the park by yourselves any more."

"But it wasn't—" Vee tries.

"I said *no buts,* Veronica."

Whoa. He only uses Vee's in-trouble name when things are *really* serious.

Dad makes us sit down right there in a patch of shade and talks about being responsible. Being fair. Playing safe. There's no point interrupting Dad when he's like this. It's like when Baby starts his hiccup wail. You can't distract him till he's finished.

We sit on the grass and listen to Dad talk. It's hot, even in the shade. I watch Messy chase his lead and then sniff the parents' bench.

There are two grown-ups sitting on the parents' bench who don't look like parents. It's a man and a woman in super smart business clothes, not paying any attention to the kids. They are talking quietly, leaning towards each other, as if what they're saying is really important. Our noisy playground is a funny place for super smart business grown-ups to come and talk seriously.

"Sita, did you hear me?" Dad's voice interrupts my thoughts.

"Um. Yep," I say.

Messy is right near the bench, sniffing the woman's shoe.

"So do you promise?" Dad asks.

The woman leans down and scratches behind Messy's ears, just where he likes it.

"I promise," I say.

"No leaving anyone out," Dad says. "The **bonus sisters** are a team, and you stick together and keep each other safe. Right?"

"Right," we all agree.

"So we can come back to the park tomorrow?" I ask.

"I suppose so." Dad pushes himself up to his feet. "All right, let's get that puppy home."

"That puppy" has made a new friend. He's sitting on the businesswoman's lap, and she looks much less serious.

He's all **wriggly**, and it's making her smile.

"Messy!" I call. He jumps off her lap and sprints over to us in the sun. His floppy ears are so cute when he runs.

"Thanks for not telling Dad about the hole," I whisper to Jessie as Dad tries to catch Messy's lead and Messy dances away from him.

"What *happened* in there?" she asks.

"We found a tunnel that goes all the way to the river!" Vee says, grinning.

Jessie's eyes widen. She doesn't look happy *at all.*

The next day at school, we are learning about pollution in water. Ms Mobarak says that now is a good time to learn about it, because of the news about Zoom Mining's toxic accident.

She shows a video about toxic waste. It's like **poison**, and you have to store it carefully so it doesn't get into the water and make everyone ill. First the video scans along a big, brown river, just like our city's river, but it's in a different part of the country. Then there's a picture of a man in a neon orange top with a circle logo on his chest. He's pointing to some toxic waste.

I gasp, because I realize I've seen toxic waste before. On the video, the toxic waste is wrapped in orange plastic and stacked in a pile. *Exactly like the pile in the tunnel.*

Then the video goes to a boring part about picking up rubbish and dog poo to stop it from going down the drain. As soon as the video ends, I throw my hand in the air.

Ms Mobarak looks at me. "Yes, Squishy?" (Even my teachers call me that.)

"Would you be allowed to store toxic waste under the city?" I ask.

"No." Ms Mobarak shakes her head, smiling at me. "That would be against the law."

I think about the pile in the tunnel and the angry man we saw. "So if Zoom Mining stored the toxic waste under the city, would they be criminals?" I ask.

She nods, opening her mouth to answer.

"And then they would have to go to prison, right?" I say quickly.

Ms Mobarak isn't smiling any more. "That's right, Squishy, but no one is storing toxic waste under the city." She turns to the rest of the class. "Now, who noticed the part where –"

"But the city river *is* polluted," I interrupt. "We're not allowed to swim in it. So someone must be storing toxic waste somewhere."

"Yes, the river is polluted, but that's a little different from –"

"Ms Mobarak, *how* is it different?"

"I think that's enough, Squishy. It's time to let everyone else do some talking."

I bite my tongue and let them talk about dog poo. I know something no one else knows. An angry man from Zoom Mining is hiding toxic waste in a tunnel under the city.

Chapter Six

After school, we dump our bags in the kitchen. **It's so hot**. We grab cartons of frozen juice from the freezer and head straight back out the door. Our apartment is on the eleventh floor, so we have to wait for the lift.

"There's a secret toxic-waste dump under the city," I say, because Jessie still doesn't believe me. I've already described the video while we were on the bus, but

Jessie just snorted. Jessie only trusts *some* types of evidence, and that doesn't include trusting what I tell her.

"It's not a toxic-waste dump," Jessie says in her **boring grown-up voice**, standing beside the lift door.

"It is, and if we fixed it, we could all swim in the river," I say, sucking juice around the ice in my carton.

Vee looks at me with bright eyes. "Imagine if we could swim in the river!"

"We could jump and dive off the bridge," I say.

Vee laughs and says, "We could climb underneath the bridge with no harness, and if we fell we'd just fall in the river."

Vee is a genius.

We high-five and laugh loudly.

Then our next-door neighbour's door opens. He steps out, striding towards the lift. Our next-door neighbour is the **grumpiest man** in the universe. His name is Mr Hinkenbushel, and sometimes he gets so angry that he spits. He hates it when we make noise. Actually, he probably hates it even when all we do is *breathe*.

I think he's going to shout at us for laughing in the corridor. But he doesn't. The lift dings, and he steps into it with us.

We stand there in silence as the lift doors slowly close. Mr Hinkenbushel ignores us and stares straight ahead. Vee elbows me, and I try not to giggle. Jessie tries to be cool, and takes a sip of her juice, but it makes a funny slurping noise. I **choke** on my laughter.

Then I think of something. Mr Hinkenbushel isn't just our grumpy neighbour. He's also an undercover police officer.

"Um, Mr Hinkenbushel?" I begin.

"What?" he snaps. He looks at me like I'm a slug.

"Did you know someone from Zoom Mining is breaking the law, right near our playground?"

"What?" he snaps again. Only now his eyes are interested. "What kind of law?"

This is weird, because he never asks questions. He never wants kids to talk.

"One about pollution–" I start as the lift stops. The doors open.

"How do you *know*?" he asks, looking at me as we walk into the entrance hall.

Then Jessie steps in. "She doesn't *know* anything," she says. "She's just making things up."

I can't believe it. Jessie used her adult voice to team up against me with *Mr Hinkenbushel*. **Our sworn enemy**. The grumpiest man in the universe. My tummy feels sick with anger.

"I do know stuff, *Jessica*," I say. "You think you're so–"

I stop myself from saying something *really* mean and stride through the hall. The sun beats off the pavement outside and feels as angry as my insides.

Jessie and Vee jog after me. Jessie is at my shoulder, trying to sound reasonable. "But you *are* making it up, Squishy," she says.

Today Jessie is *not* a bonus.

Behind us, Mr Hinkenbushel is proving that he's still the grumpiest man in the universe. He shouts, "Hey, you kids! Don't make up lies about crime. It's a stupid thing to do. And if you think someone's a criminal, *steer clear of them*. Don't be nosy fools."

I bet he's **spitting** too. He always spits when he shouts. I don't look. I don't even care.

When we get to the playground, I head straight towards the tall patch of grass where we first lost Messy.

"Squishy, where are you going?" Jessie asks. "Squishy, you can't go down there. We promised–"

"I just want to *look*," I say. It's like she's from another planet. How could you know there's a secret tunnel under your city and not at least go and look at the entrance?

"Fine," she says.

The cover is back on tight. We all stare down at it. There isn't really much to see.

It's too hot on the playground to actually play. There aren't many kids. We sprawl in the shade, sucking our juices. I make a point of ignoring Jessie.

"I wish Messy was here," I say to Vee.

"Imagine if we could swim in the river," Vee says.

I notice that smart business couple is here again. They're talking in the same way they were yesterday. Like what they're saying is very important.

"What do you think those people are doing?" I ask, nodding towards the couple.

"Looking after kids," Vee says.

But Jessie shakes her head. "All three of the kids in the playground have another grown-up with them."

She is *good with evidence,* I think grudgingly. Just not so good with trust.

Jessie is staring at them, looking really interested. "Why are they sitting in the sun?" she asks. "It looks pretty uncomfortable."

Then Vee gasps and points in the other direction. "Hey, look!"

The man from the tunnel has just arrived in the park. He's carrying a heavy-looking rucksack. He walks straight to the tall grass and bends over to shift the cover. In a couple of minutes, he has disappeared under the city.

"See," I say. "Neon Guy is carrying more waste down there in his rucksack."

"Squishy!" Jessie laughs. "People don't carry toxic waste in rucksacks!"

"How do you *know?*" I ask.

"They just don't," Jessie says. "He's probably going down to fix the drains."

"Then what's *he* doing?" Vee asks. She points across the street.

Mr Hinkenbushel is leaning against a building, watching our park with a pair of binoculars.

Our local undercover police officer is spying on our playground. And there are more grown-ups here than kids. Something is **definitely** going on in that tunnel.

Chapter Seven

After school, I grab the iPad and sprawl on my belly on the living room floor. It's time to Skype Mum. Mum has a big job in Geneva, Switzerland, which is why I don't live with her any more. Sometimes I miss her so much I can't breathe, but lots of the time there's too many other fun, weird adventures to think about.

Mum's face comes up on the screen. She's behind her desk in her United

Nations office. She grins at me. "Hey, **Squishy-sweet**. Did you see Messy today?" she asks. I Skype her every day, so she already knows all my big news. Except the tunnel. That's a secret even from her.

"Nah. Hey, Mum, pollution is really bad, right?"

Mum smiles, because she likes that I get straight to the point. "Some pollution is very, very bad, and some is just a little bit bad. But even the little bits add up," Mum says. She never just says yes or no.

"But what Zoom Mining did was *illegal*," I push.

Mum knows all about it because she reads loads of newspapers every day. "Maybe," she says. "*If* they deliberately did things they knew could cause a spill. We'll find that out soon."

"But if it's against the law," I say, "why would they do it?"

Mum is a good answerer. She looks at me with her **thinking face**. "Great question, Squishy. Maybe because they can make more money taking risks. It costs more money to do everything carefully and obey the law."

"Until you have to pay huge amounts of money to clean up toxic waste," I say.

Mum grins at me. "Exactly, Squishy. Unless you can get away with pretending it wasn't your fault."

Vee jumps over the sofa and lands, **like a horse rider**, on my back. She squashes my shoulders with her elbows and leans in to look at the screen. "Hi, Devika!"

"Hi, Vee." Mum smiles.

Jessie brings Baby over, and we laugh at his big gummy smile when he sees Mum. Baby doesn't know Mum is a person. He thinks she lives inside the iPad.

I want to tell Mum about the secret toxic-waste dump. It's burning in my chest. But I can't tell her without explaining how we went down in the tunnel. I watch her do **cutesy-face** at Baby, who is waving his arms like crazy.

I think about the toxic waste in the tunnel. Jessie still doesn't believe it's down there. What would make her believe me?

As soon as I think the question, I know the answer. Google would make Jessie believe me. I pull the iPad off Jessie.

"I miss you, Squisho," Mum says.

"Miss you too." I press the hang-up button and roll over.

"Dad?" I call. "Can I Google something?"

Our iPad is set up so the only app that goes online without a password is Skype. Once we used the iPad to make a **revenge website** about Mr Hinkenbushel. Another time we hacked security footage, but then we got caught. Now the iPad is only to talk to Mum, unless we ask.

"What do you want to Google?" Dad asks from the kitchen.

"Toxic waste. We learned about it at school today."

Jessie makes a face as I take the iPad over to the sink. Dad peels off his big yellow rubber gloves and drapes them on the sink edge. Then he types in the password.

"Thanks!"

I Google *toxic waste* and get a news video. I watch it, walking back to the sofa.

"*A massive clean-up operation is underway,*" says the voice-over. "*Zoom Mining denies any illegal activity. They claim they always stayed within government safety standards. This would make taxpayers responsible for the clean-up bill. An investigation has begun–*"

An investigation. Sounds interesting, but it's not what I'm looking for.

The toxic-waste video from school is a few videos down. I tap it while Jessie and Vee look over my shoulder. When the orange plastic comes up, I pause the video.

Vee gasps. "That's what we saw in the

tunnel, Jessie. Exactly it."

"Shhh," I say, glancing over at Dad's back. He doesn't turn around.

We all stare at the iPad with its picture of orange plastic.

Jessie looks like she's going to say something about why we're wrong.

Vee leans in and hisses, "Seriously, Jessie. It's *exactly* the same."

She waves her arm as she says "exactly", and Baby's face gets in the way. He falls over backwards, and his head goes *bump* on the floor.

Darn.

He screws up his face. "Waaaaaah!"

Now they'll notice it's bedtime.

Alice steps out of their room. "Bedtime, everyone!" she says. "Get a move on."

Alice picks up Baby and bounces him, which makes his wail go up and down like a police siren.

I'm pulling my pyjamas on when Jessie comes into our room. She's got something under her top.

Jessie grins at me and slides the iPad out. "It's still unlocked," she says. "If they don't notice I've taken it, we might be able to get to the bottom of this tonight."

Chapter Eight

Once the lights are out, Vee does a **rolling-spin-drop** from her top bunk to my middle one. Then she goes again, down to Jessie's on the bottom, and I follow. We huddle around the iPad, hushing each other and trying not to giggle.

Jessie has opened a news article about the investigation.

I use my best dramatic whisper to sum up what we're all thinking. "So Neon

Guy from the park works for Zoom Mining. He's dumping toxic waste, and Mr Hinkenbushel is investigating him. That's what the news was about."

Jessie **wrinkles** her face, pointing at the article. "The investigation in the news isn't about a new dump. It's about whether Zoom Mining was breaking the law before the big spill."

"Well, if they're dumping toxic waste under the city, that's breaking the law," I say. "That must be why an undercover police officer is staking out the entrance to the tunnel."

"You should come down with us," Vee whispers to Jessie. "It's the coolest tunnel. Then you'd see the toxic waste, and you'd believe us."

Jessie shakes her head. "There's no *way* I'm going down there."

"But Jessie–" Vee starts.

"No, Vee! It's *so* dangerous!" Jessie's voice is loud.

"**Shhh**," I say, and we all look at the door.

Nothing. They didn't hear us.

Jessie hunches her shoulders and taps something in the search bar. She's so fast, I can't even read over her shoulder.

"That's it," she whispers as the list of search results comes up. "That's the section with our park." She taps the third result down on the list.

A strange map comes up. It looks like a normal map, except there are a whole lot of extra grey lines criss-crossing the roads.

"What are the grey lines?" Vee asks, leaning in closer.

"Tunnels," I whisper, grinning as I realize what the map shows.

Jessie points to a dot on the line in a green section. "Here's our park. And if you got to the river, you must have gone . . ." Her finger glides along a line, as if she's following a maze. ". . . here." She stops where the line reaches a bigger blue line, which must be the river. Our river is brown, not blue, but the map people probably don't know that.

Jessie zooms in so we can see more. She points to our street. Then she reads something at the bottom of the map.

"Warning! Workers are advised never to enter drainage tunnels during wet weather as drains may flood suddenly."

"**Shhh!**" Vee says.

We hear Dad. "The kids had it just before, on the floor by the sofa."

I hold my breath. They've discovered that the iPad is missing.

Footsteps move around, and I hear the noise of the sofa being dragged slightly.

"Go, go, go!" Vee whispers.

We both do **kicking-two-jump-scrambles** up to our bunks and bury ourselves under our blankets.

Just in time.

The door cracks open, and I peek. Alice stands with the light of the kitchen behind her.

Jessie is doing amazing sleep-breathing.

Alice tiptoes towards us and leans over Jessie. I shift as quietly as I can so I can see what's happening underneath me. Alice is sliding the iPad out from under Jessie's sleepy-floppy hand. She sighs and stands up.

I mumble and roll over to disguise the fact that I was peering over the edge of the bunk at her.

As soon as Alice closes the door, we all burst into shaking, silent laughter.

"That was *so* close!" whispers Vee.

"Nice acting, Jessie," I say.

"I even closed the map image before she came in," Jessie says.

I've got my duvet in my mouth to stop the laughter from coming out. But then I remember we still have a problem.

"We're still no closer to working out what to do about the toxic waste," I say.

Jessie rolls over underneath me. "Squishy, you don't know it's toxic waste."

"But Mr Hinkenbushel is *investigating* it. It's *got* to be. He needs to know where

Neon Guy is dumping the waste," I say. "We've got to tell him."

The others are silent. I think about Mr Hinkenbushel looking at me as if I'm a slug and yelling so hard he spits.

After a pause, I say, "I'm going to do it. I'm going to knock on his door in the morning."

Chapter Nine

In the morning, I grab my toast and go and stand in front of Mr Hinkenbushel's door. Before anyone can stop me. Before I get too scared.

I take a big bite and then knock.

He answers immediately and does his *I'm-looking-at-a-slug* face. I try to swallow my toast but can't. As soon as I start talking, his face turns red. And it's not just because some **half-chewed**

toast fell out of my mouth. He really doesn't like what I'm saying.

"Kid, get this into your head!" Mr Hinkenbushel shouts at me. "You don't know *anything*. Anything you *think* you know is wrong." His voice is booming in the corridor, and I'm scared Dad and Alice will hear. We promised not to bother him.

Mr Hinkenbushel leans forward and spits, "You're getting in the way of a police investigation."

Talking to Mr Hinkenbushel is pretty much the worst idea I ever had.

"What is going *on*?" Dad asks, poking his head out of our front door.

"Mr Taylor, will you please tell your snooping kid to keep her meddling nose out of my business? She's going to get herself into big trouble."

Dad sighs and puts his hand on my shoulder. He marches me away.

"Squishy," he tells me, "I know you're curious, but you seriously need to stay clear of Mr Hinkenbushel."

On the bus ride to school, I make up my mind. "We have to go down there," I say.

Vee nods.

"No *way*," Jessie says.

"But we *have* to," I say. "We're the only ones who know."

"You don't know *anything*," Jessie says, sounding exactly like Mr Hinkenbushel.

"Neon Guy is dumping Zoom Mining's toxic waste. We've got a responsibility to get to the bottom of it." The bus is **sticky-hot** because the air-conditioning is broken. It's so weird how hot it's been. And it makes it harder to think.

Jessie folds her arms. "I am not going," she declares. "And you're not going without me."

"Oh, *come on,* Jess," Vee says.

"No. It's too dangerous. We promised Tom we'd be a team. We promised we'd never leave anyone alone."

"You won't be alone," Vee says, after a moment. "You'll be with Messy."

Genius. No one's alone when they're with Messy.

I grin at Jessie, who looks pale.

"It would be much better to know the truth, wouldn't it?" I say.

Jessie's into facts and the truth. She tightens her lips.

After school, we get ready as quickly as we can.

I'm not an idiot. I know you shouldn't touch toxic waste, so I get Dad's yellow rubber gloves from under the sink. They're really big, but they'll do.

Vee grabs the torch from where it's always kept, in the second drawer down. I take the kitchen scissors. I need something to cut the rope tying down the plastic if it's too tight.

The only other thing we need is the iPad, for photographing evidence. Luckily Dad left it charging by the TV, so Vee brings it over.

While I'm shoving everything in my rucksack, Jessie clutches a piece of paper. It's the map we were looking at yesterday.

"You printed it?" I ask.

She nods, still a little pale. "In the library at lunchtime. So I can show a rescue party where you are."

"We won't need a rescue party," I say.

"I still don't think you should go," she replies.

"Can we go and get Messy now?" Vee asks as Alice steps into the room. We need a grown-up to take us to puppy school.

Finally we're in the park, and Alice has gone home. Messy is bouncing at our knees with his tongue hanging out of his mouth. He's **so cute** it makes my chest hurt.

It's still pretty hot outside, but luckily the sun isn't beating down any more. Instead there are big, dark clouds rolling across the sky. They look like they're from the set of a scary film.

Jessie is still really quiet, but she's not trying to stop us any more. "Are you all ready?" she asks.

Vee nods. I pull my rucksack on tighter. Messy licks my kneecap.

I look around the park. Neon Guy is nowhere to be seen. Mr Hinkenbushel is across the street with his binoculars, but he seems distracted. He's watching the business couple, who are back on the bench. He's not watching the tunnel entrance at all. Lucky we're doing his job for him.

We walk to the tunnel entrance and push away the cover as a team.

Vee heads down into the dark. I give Messy one last scratch behind the ears and nod at Jessie.

As I start to climb down the hole, a **drop of rain** lands on the end of my nose.

Chapter Ten

It doesn't take long to reach the cavern this time. At the end of our tunnel, where it opens up, I shrug off the rucksack and kneel down to rummage through it. Gloves first. Then torch. It's hard to turn on the torch with my big rubbery fingers, so I pass it to Vee.

"What's that?" Vee asks, looking around nervously, as though she's heard something.

"What's what?" I reply, walking towards the toxic waste with Vee beside me. I'm thinking about the fact that we're about to prove someone is committing a huge environmental crime.

"**Footsteps**," Vee says, "coming down that other tunnel."

I pause. She's right. I can hear footsteps too, coming from the far tunnel. That means we only have a minute to find out the truth. I bolt over to the plastic pile as fast as I can. We need this evidence. And we need it now.

The plastic is tied down tight. I scramble around it, looking for a loose place. None. Lucky I brought scissors. **There!** I snip a few sections free, and the whole thing comes loose like a big net. I shove the scissors back into my rucksack, throw the rope aside and peel the plastic back to look.

It's not toxic waste at all.

"Squishy, hurry, they're getting closer," Vee says. She's at my side now, with the torch. "Oh," she says, looking at what was under the plastic. A shopping trolley, a stack of tools and a neat pile of bricks. Beside them are some bags of cement and a cement mixer.

Neon Guy runs into the cavern. "Kids! What are you *doing*? You *really* shouldn't be here."

I stare at the circle logo on his top. This is the first time he's been close enough for me to read it. The logo isn't for Zoom Mining at all. It says *Drainz R Us*.

"You're . . . you're just fixing the drains," I say. That's what Jessie said he was doing.

"Of *course* I am, why else would I be down here? Listen, it's raining cats and dogs. It's going to get **dangerous** quickly. We have to run."

If it's raining that bad, Jessie will be getting soaked waiting for us. And Alice will expect us to come home. He's right. We should run. I turn back towards our tunnel.

"Squishy! We can't go that way," Vee says, pointing. "Look."

She's right. Our tiny trickle of a stream has filled up already. It's covering our path. I remember that warning Jessie read to us when we were looking at the drain map. Something about sudden floods.

Something about it being dangerous to work down here when it's raining.

"Quick! Downstream," Neon Guy says, gesturing for us to go first. "Go, go, go!"

We run towards the tunnel to the river. Me first, then Vee and finally Neon Guy. As we run, the stream gets more and more full. At first there are trickles over the walkway. Then wide puddles. Then we're running ankle-deep in water.

I keep thinking I hear splashing footsteps a long way behind us. It must just be the way we echo in the tunnel.

I trip over something in the dark and land face-first in the stream.

I'm still wearing those stupid plastic gloves, and they fill with water, feeling

cold around my fingers. I scramble back to my feet and peel them off as I run. The water is up to my knees as I throw the gloves away from me. I can hear Vee crying as she runs.

I have never been this scared in my life. I feel something against my legs. Something slithery in the water. I **scream**. And then I realize it's the net that tied the orange plastic, being washed downstream. I kick it aside and keep running.

Finally we're at the entrance. I scramble a few steps up the bank. It's raining heavily, but I don't care.

Jessie is here. She's kneeling by the river, holding a yellow rubber glove, and crying. She doesn't even notice me.

It's Messy who sees me first. He leaps into my arms, barking and licking my face. I clutch him, half-laughing, half-crying.

Jessie hears him and turns around as Vee scrambles up beside us. Jessie's face lights up. Neon Guy is behind Vee, at the tunnel entrance. He's up to his hips in water.

Jessie hugs Vee, their black hair merging so you can't tell whose is whose. "I thought you'd drowned!" Jessie says into Vee's shoulder.

I think about the fact that we nearly did drown. **Jessie was right**. We should never have gone down there. I squeeze Messy tighter and start to feel sick thinking about it. Messy licks my face even more, as if he can tell how bad I feel.

When Neon Guy reaches the path beside us, Jessie pulls back from the hug and asks, "Where's Mr Hinkenbushel?"

"What?" Vee asks.

Jessie looks worried. "Didn't you see him?"

"No, why would we?"

"He saw you go down and followed you in. He was worried about flash-flooding." Jessie half-smiles, but her face is really pale. "He was right to be worried. I gave him the map, and he said he'd bring you out this way. He said he'd find you and meet me here."

Those footsteps I heard. He must have been behind us.

Just then Messy turns in my arms and growls down at the tunnel entrance. Right afterwards, I hear a voice booming out.

"Help! Help! I'm stuck!"

It's Mr Hinkenbushel.

Chapter Eleven

"My leg's tangled. I can't get it free!" Mr Hinkenbushel is by the tunnel entrance, struggling in the water. Messy leaps out of my arms and runs to the water's edge. He barks **wildly** at Mr Hinkenbushel, who lifts something above the surface. It's part of the rope net I kicked aside. The water is almost up to his armpits. It's brown with white foam on it, rushing into the river.

The Neon Guy leans over and reaches for Mr Hinkenbushel's hand. He pulls hard, but nothing happens. Mr Hinkenbushel stays stuck, and Messy keeps on barking.

"It's no use," Mr Hinkenbushel says. "I'm too tangled."

Neon Guy scrambles past Messy down into the rough water. He plunges his head under, near Mr Hinkenbushel, and we wait. He comes up puffing.

"Can't get it," he says. I can see the ends of the net lashing around in the current. Neon Guy takes another deep breath and goes under again. We stand on the edge, watching both men kick and flail. I lift up Messy and cuddle him, trying to get him to calm down, but he squirms against me, barking like there's no tomorrow.

Their heads come up again.

"Oh, no! Now *I'm* caught!" shouts Neon Guy. He struggles to get free, but he can't.

Two grown-ups are tangled in the water, and we're stuck on the bank, watching them. We can't go in there. The river would just wash us away.

"If only we had a knife!" Jessie says.

Jessie's right again. And I feel stupid. I've got scissors.

I drop Messy on the grass and whip the kitchen scissors out of my rucksack.

"Here!" I shout and then pass them carefully, handles first, to Neon Guy. He grabs them.

In seconds, both men are on the bank. Soaking wet. But not drowning.

"Thanks, kid," Neon Guy says, passing the scissors back to me. "You saved our lives."

"They should've stayed out of danger in the first place," Mr Hinkenbushel mutters. Messy leaps up and tries to lick his knees, nearly knocking him back into the water. But Messy's tail is wagging, and Mr Hinkenbushel leans over and gives him a rough pat.

Vee's lips are blue, and my teeth are chattering. It's still raining big, heavy drops.

"Everyone needs to get home and dry," Neon Guy says. "And someone needs to talk to your parents."

My stomach cramps up. Dad and Alice can't know what we've been doing. We'd never be allowed to leave our bedroom again.

We all scramble up the path and start walking home through the wet city streets.

Messy and Neon Guy make friends. Neon Guy scratches behind Messy's ears, and Messy **bounces** around him. Vee explains about Messy being ours but not really.

I don't talk. I'm feeling scared of what Dad will say when we get home. The more I think about it, the more I realize Jessie was right, and it was stupid to go in that tunnel. I keep remembering all that raging water rushing into the river.

But I'm walking beside Mr Hinkenbushel, and I can't help being curious. When we're waiting to cross the street, I finally open my mouth.

"Mr Hinkenbushel, if you weren't staking out Neon Guy, what *were* you doing?"

Mr Hinkenbushel frowns. "Kid, when are you gonna learn that it's none of your–"

But before he can say anything else, something happens. Messy stops jumping around Neon Guy's feet and **bolts** over to the entrance of a bank.

"Messy, stop it. Here boy!" Vee shouts.

Messy jumps up to the knees of a smart businesswoman standing on the steps of a bank. The woman laughs and pushes Messy down. It's that same businesswoman from the park.

Then she frowns. "Hey, bad dog. Drop that! Give it back! No!"

Messy is **bolting** towards us with something in his teeth. He takes it straight to Jessie, who is holding out a treat from her pocket.

"Good boy. Drop it. There's a good boy."

Messy drops a USB stick from his mouth into Jessie's hand. She stares down at it.

"Give that back," the woman says, running towards us in the rain. She doesn't seem so friendly any more. She looks angry. And maybe even scared. She wasn't wearing that lanyard in the park.

I look over Jessie's shoulder. The USB stick has Zoom Mining's logo on it.

Chapter Twelve

I snatch the USB from Jessie for a closer look. It definitely has the Zoom Mining logo. The label on it says *secret safety records.*

Jessie looks at the woman sternly. "Are these the safety records you're hiding from the police?"

I can't believe Jessie is doing her **big sister voice** on a grown-up. Jessie is *so cool.*

The woman looks like Vee does when she's been caught sneaking chocolate. "It's got nothing to do with you," the woman says. Then she turns to me. "Give it back."

I clutch the USB in my fist behind my back and lean against the wall, squashing my hand.

Messy **dances** in front of me like we're about to play fetch with the USB stick. I think about how angry that would make the Zoom Mining lady and almost do it, just for fun.

"You weren't watching the tunnel in our park at all, were you, Mr Hinkenbushel?" Jessie says. "You were watching the Zoom Mining lady getting secret information!"

I can't believe she's talking like this.

Mr Hinkenbushel nods at Jessie and turns to me. "And now I think you'd better give that to me," he says.

I'm about to give it to him. He is a police officer, after all. But then I clutch the USB tighter. I've thought of something. "If I give this to you, will you promise not to tell Dad and Alice what we did today?"

Neon Guy bursts into laughter. "What a wacky group of kids you are."

Mr Hinkenbushel goes red. Then he mutters, "I promise."

Zoom Lady is trying to **dodge** around to get to my hand, but Messy and Vee stand in her way. Messy isn't so friendly to her any more. He's growling.

I think about Mr Hinkenbushel's muttering. It doesn't sound like a real promise. I think if Jessie can do her **big sister voice** to a grown-up, I can too.

"Mr Hinkenbushel, say it like you mean it," I insist, like Dad does when he's making me say sorry. It comes out sounding pretty convincing, and I feel proud of myself. Then I think of something even better. "Actually, **pinkie-promise** with Jessie."

"Fine. Whatever." Mr Hinkenbushel turns even redder, but he links little pinkie fingers with Jessie.

"Now repeat after me," I say. "I pinkie-promise not to tell Tom and Alice–"

"I pinkie-promise not to tell Tom and Alice," Mr Hinkenbushel mutters.

"That we went down a drain and almost died," I finish.

"That we went down a drain and almost died," he copies me, looking really embarrassed.

"Good," I say. I nod and hand him the USB.

Neon Guy grins. Zoom Lady turns pale.

Mr Hinkenbushel turns to Zoom Lady. "You'll be hearing from me and the Undercover Operations Unit as soon as I am able to take a thorough look at these files," he says to her, waving the USB stick. "But first I have to lie to some parents."

He **scowls** at me. But he doesn't quite look like the grumpiest man in the universe any more.

Dad laughs at us and calls us **drowned rats**. He doesn't even blink when we say we got caught in the rain. He shakes Mr Hinkenbushel's hand and calls Messy's kennel to let them know he'll be spending the night with us.

We take hot showers and put our pyjamas on, even though it's not bedtime. Alice makes hot chocolate, and we all sit on Jessie's bunk with a blanket wrapped around us. Messy curls up on my lap.

I've still got a knot in my stomach, because there's something I have to say to Jessie.

"Jessie, you were *so* right about not going down the tunnel," I tell her. "It was *so* dangerous. And you were *so* cool with Zoom Lady. I'm sorry for not listening."

Jessie actually blushes. "I was feeling bad for not being brave enough to go down there with you."

I stare at her. *Jessie* was feeling bad? Jessie didn't go because she wasn't *brave* enough?

Vee bursts out laughing.

"What?" Jessie and I say at the same time.

"You both felt bad, but actually you were being a good team," Vee says. "Joke's on you."

We all crack up.

Just then, the sound of the news from the living room catches our attention.

"In breaking news, police have uncovered information in the Zoom Mining case. A large number of secret files recording

the mine's unsafe practices have found their way into the hands of the police."

I grin. "Found their way?" I say. "More like: were discovered by a **team of super ninjas** and traded for a lifetime of police loyalty!"

Messy jumps up and barks proudly, and we all laugh and clink mugs.

The newsreader is talking about something else by the time we finish gleefully **cheers-ing** each other with our hot chocolates.

"There's something I don't understand, though," Vee says.

"What?" we ask.

"If the Zoom Mining woman really is the bad guy, how come Messy liked her?

Don't dogs always know who the bad guy is?"

I pull Messy in towards me and rub behind his ears. I remember the businesswoman smiling as she made friends with him on the park bench. "Yeah, and she seemed so nice," I say.

"Maybe she's only eighty-five per cent bad, and the other fifteen per cent likes dogs," Jessie says.

"And maybe," Vee says, "Messy knew that he'd get that USB by being friendly."

Messy wags his tail and licks her nose.

"Probably." I nod, and then we all laugh because we know it's not true.

I lean against the wall and sip my hot chocolate. I feel a little sad that the adventure is over.

"What are we going to do now?" I ask.

"We don't have long before Messy goes home," Jessie says. "Maybe I'll actually try playing Dog Tag tomorrow."

"Woo!" Vee says, and does a **kicking-two-jump-scramble** up to her bunk.

She knocks Messy on the way, who does a **howling half-somersault** back onto the mattress.

He knocks my hot chocolate, which goes flying in a big brown arc. All over Jessie's duvet.

THE END
—

About the author and illustrator

Ailsa Wild is an acrobat, whip-cracker and teaching artist who ran away from the circus to become a writer. She taught Squishy all her best bunk-bed tricks.

Ben Wood started drawing when he was Baby's age and happily drew all over his mum and dad's walls! Since then, he has never stopped drawing. He has an identical twin, and they used to play all kinds of pranks on their younger brother.

Author acknowledgements

Christy and Luke, for writing residencies, bunk-bed acrobatics, and the day you turned the truck around.

Antoni, Penni, Moreno and the masterclass crew, for showing me what the journey could be. Here's to epiphanies.

Indira and Devika, because she couldn't be real without you.

Hilary, Marisa, Penny, Sarah and the HGE team, for making it happen. What an amazing net to have landed in.

Ben, for bringing them all to life.

Jono, for independence and supporting each other's dreams.

– Ailsa

Illustrator acknowledgements

Hilary, Marisa, Sarah and the HGE team, for your enthusiasm and spark.

Penny, for being the best! Thanks for inviting me along on this Squish-tastic ride! (And for putting up with all my emails!)

Ailsa, for creating such a fun place for me to play in.

John, for listening to me ramble on and on about Squishy Taylor every day.

– Ben

Talk about it!

1. Squishy, Vee and Jessie are looking after Carmeline Clancy's dog, Messy, for her. Do you think they're doing a good job? Discuss what they do well and what they could do better.

2. Squishy and her bonus sisters keep secrets from their parents in this story. Do you think they did the right thing by keeping their secrets?

3. When Squishy and Vee go into the hole to rescue Messy, Jessie stays behind. Do you think Jessie was right not to follow them? What would you have done in her situation?

Write about it!

1. In this story, Squishy sets out to discover if there is toxic waste being dumped in her city. Write about pollution you've seen or heard about in your life.

2 Neon Guy ends up being innocent in this story. Imagine Neon Guy was the person in the wrong, rather than Zoom Lady, and write a different ending to this story.

3. What do you think Mr Hinkenbushel might find in the secret files that Zoom Mining Lady was protecting? From Mr Hinkenbushel's perspective, write a summary of what he finds.

For more exciting books from
brilliant authors, check out our website!

www.raintree.co.uk